INTRODUCING

Funny
Fool

Blue
the
Brave

Pete

Casper

For Jonathan
C.C.

For Jack, Jamie and Jessie,
with love and a big yeehah! xx
J.McC.

Reading Consultant: Prue Goodwin, Lecturer in literacy and children's books

ORCHARD BOOKS
338 Euston Road, London NW1 3BH
Orchard Books Australia
Hachette Children's Books
Level 17/207 Kent Street, Sydney NSW 2000

First published in 2011 by Orchard Books
First paperback publication in 2012

Text © Catherine Coe 2011
Illustrations © Jan McCafferty 2011

ISBN 978 1 40830 688 8 (hardback)
ISBN 978 1 40830 696 3 (paperback)

1 3 5 7 9 10 8 6 4 2 (hardback)
1 3 5 7 9 10 8 6 4 2 (paperback)

Printed in China

Orchard Books is a division of Hachette Children's Books,
an Hachette UK company.

www.hachette.co.uk

School Scare

Written by
Catherine Coe **Illustrated by**
Jan McCafferty

ORCHARD

Casper the Kid Cowboy and his best friend, Pete, couldn't believe it. It was the holidays, but tomorrow they had to go to summer school!

"It isn't fair," Casper said to Pete. "I want to do cowboy things like ride across the Wild West all day. School isn't for cowboys!"
Pete agreed.

They spent the afternoon trying
to do as many fun things as
they could.

The next morning, Casper and
Pete set off for Ranchland
Summer School, feeling gloomy.

But their horses, Blue the Brave and Funny Fool, trotted along happily. They didn't seem to mind going to school!

Casper, Pete, Blue and Funny Fool
arrived at the school gates.
But there was a problem. The
horses wouldn't fit!

"Come on, Blue," Casper said to his horse, trying to squeeze him through the gates. But it was no good. The cowboys had to leave their beloved horses outside. "So long!" they shouted.

There were lots of other horses
waiting outside, too. Blue and
Funny Fool quickly made friends.

Suddenly a cowbell rang loudly. Casper and Pete rushed to their first lesson.

It was Art. They had to draw
their favourite animals.
"I'll draw Blue and Funny
Fool," Casper said to Pete.
"I'll draw lots of cows,"
said Pete.

Pete had put his hat on his peg. Casper wanted to keep his hat on – but it kept getting in the way. It almost got covered in green paint. Pete was painting a *lot* of grass.

"I'll have to take off my hat,"
Casper decided. "Just for
a minute."

The teacher looked after Casper's
hat. The two cowboys finished
their pictures.

"Excellent work, boys," the teacher said.

Next it was P.E.

"Yee-ha," Pete said when he saw the basketball court. "This might be fun!"

Casper took his lasso outside.
He thought it might help – but
instead it just got in the way.
He kept falling over!

"Shall I look after it for you?"
the P.E. teacher asked.

"OK," said Casper, slowly
nodding his head.

Basketball became a *lot* more fun. Casper even shot a hoop!

At break time, Casper missed his hat and his lasso. But most of all he missed Blue. It seemed that none of his cowboy things belonged at school.

"I don't feel like a real cowboy any more," Casper told Pete.

But Pete had an idea. "We can still *play* cowboys!"
Soon the whole class was pretending to ride horses and swing lassos.

Suddenly things didn't seem
so bad. And Casper was a *very*
good pretend cowboy!

"I suppose deep down I'll *always* be a cowboy," he said to Pete, "whatever I look like." "You sure will, partner!" Pete replied.

At the end of the day, Casper got his hat and lasso back. He smiled as he saw Blue waiting for him outside the school gates.

Pete and Casper rode home
with their new school friends
beside them.

They were soon back at their
treehouse hide-out.

"School wasn't too bad," Pete
admitted.

"We *did* make lots of new
friends," Casper said.
They were pinning up the
pictures they'd painted.

Then Pete fixed a basketball
hoop to the tree.
As the sun set, the cowboys
practised their new skills.

Casper had to admit that
perhaps school *was* for
cowboys. But just sometimes!

KID COWBOY

Written by
Catherine Coe

Illustrated by
Jan McCafferty

All priced at £8.99

Orchard Books are available from all good bookshops,
or can be ordered from our website: www.orchardbooks.co.uk,
or telephone 01235 827702, or fax 01235 827703.

Prices and availability are subject to change.